AN ACROSTIC FOR YOU

A Treasury Of Verse

Edited By Vicki Skelton

First published in Great Britain in 2021 by:

Young Writers
Remus House
Coltsfoot Drive
Peterborough
PE2 9BF
Telephone: 01733 890066
Website: www.youngwriters.co.uk

Book Design by Ashley Janson

Softback ISBN 978-1-80015-224-3

Printed and bound in the UK by BookPrintingUK
Website: www.bookprintinguk.com
YB0458M

Foreword

Dear Reader,

Welcome to a fun-filled book of acrostic poems!

Here at Young Writers, we are delighted to introduce our new poetry competition for pupils aged 5-7 years, An Acrostic For You. Acrostic poems are an enjoyable way to introduce pupils to the world of poetry and allow the young writers to open their imaginations to a range of topics of their choice. The engaging worksheets allowed even the youngest (or most reluctant) of writers to create a poem using the acrostic technique, and with that, encouraged them to include other literary techniques such as similes and description. Here at Young Writers we are passionate about introducing the love and art of creative writing to the next generation and we love being a part of their journey.

From family to teachers, from pets to popstars, these pupils have shaped and crafted their ideas brilliantly, showcasing their budding creativity as they celebrate the people that are important to them. More than ever it's important to show our appreciation to the people who do so much for us, and these young poets are a shining example of how to do just that. We hope you will delight in these poems as much as we have.

Contents

The Poems

Coca The Cat

C ute
O n the house
C uddly
A lways nice

T iny
H uggly
E xcited for her food

C lean
A lovely cat
T ickly.

Claire McGoldrick (5)
Abernyte Primary School, Inchture

Mummy

M ummy cuddles
U nder the covers
M y mummy is so lovely
M y mummy is Kirsty
Y ellow is her favourite.

Theo Shields (5)
Abernyte Primary School, Inchture

Tiger The Cat

T iger stripes
I n the garden
G reen eyes
E normous
R an to the school.

Noah Bailey (7)
Abernyte Primary School, Inchture

My Little Brother

F reddie is my little brother
R unning is his favourite exercise
E very day he runs in the front room
D addy makes him laugh
D ogs are his favourite animal
I n the morning we scoot to school
E ven when we fight I still love him.

Joshua Dowd (6)
All Saints Benhilton CE Primary School, Sutton

Gymnastics

G et your leotard on
Y ou are going to have fun
M ake sure you stretch
N ow it is time for
A crobatics
S plits
T rampette
I ncredible
C artwheels
S pringboard.

Evie Collins (5)

All Saints Benhilton CE Primary School, Sutton

Evie Collins

E xciting
V ery beautiful
I ce cream
E xcellent

C lever
O utstanding
L ovely
L aughy
I ndependent
N ice
S uper.

Eryn Arton (5)

All Saints Benhilton CE Primary School, Sutton

Snowflake

S miling
N ice
O verjoyed
W onderful
F abulous
L oving
A dorable
K ind-hearted
E namoured.

Ruby Goddard (5)
All Saints Benhilton CE Primary School, Sutton

Mummy

M y mummy loves me
U nicorns are our favourite things
M y mummy lifts me up
M ummy makes us food
Y ay for my mummy.

Evelyn Pemberton (5)
All Saints Benhilton CE Primary School, Sutton

Daddy

D addy is brilliant
A mazing daddy
D addy is a builder
D addy is a chef
Y ou always make me happy, Daddy.

Emily Hin (5)
All Saints Benhilton CE Primary School, Sutton

Park

P lay with friends
A utumn makes colourful leaves
R ace in the park is fun
K ites fly when the wind comes.

Nikilan Siddharth Nagarajan (5)

All Saints Benhilton CE Primary School, Sutton

Sister

S o cute
I ncredible
S mart
T en months old
E xcited
R ose.

Kristina Nikolova (5)
All Saints Benhilton CE Primary School, Sutton

My Teacher

T eaching me
E very day
A ll the time
C lapping when I'm good
H elps me to learn
E xcited to see me
R eally smiley.

Lourenco Seidi (6)
Coed Glas Primary School, Llanishen

My Doctor

D octor helps me to hear
O h no, but that's okay
C olours of the rainbow NHS
T oday and tomorrow
O ur heroes
R eally help me.

Hasnain Bilal (6)
Coed Glas Primary School, Llanishen

My Mummy

M ummy helps me
U pstairs and downstairs
M aking me dinner
M ummy gives me hugs
Y es, I love her.

Jessica Day (6)

Coed Glas Primary School, Llanishen

Teacher

T eaches me new things
E nergetic
A lways helps me
C aring and kind
H elpful
E nsures I do my best
R eminds me to do my homework.

Aliyah Memon (6)
Essex Primary School, London

My School

S uper
C ool
H appy
O n-time
O utdoor play
L earning time.

Hamza Rakhda (5)
Essex Primary School, London

Mum

M y mother is marvellous
U nderstanding
M akes sure that I am safe.

Rufaida Belbouab (6)

Essex Primary School, London

My Sister

E njoys chocolate
D oes make me smile
I s very kind
E die makes me happy

G randma loves her
R uns all over
A sks me lots and lots
C alls my name lots
E veryone loves her so much.

Annie-Rose Brown (5)
Five Lanes Primary School, Upper Wortley

Frankie

F abulous at maths
R eally good at English
A mazing at reading
N ever makes the wrong choices
K ind and red is my favourite colour
I like school very much
E very day I go to school.

Frankie Lee (6)
Five Lanes Primary School, Upper Wortley

Daniel

D oing nice things at school
A nnoy people I don't like
N ever mean to people
I like going to school
E very day I like playing with other kids
L ovely, I like playing with kids.

Daniel Toft (6)

Five Lanes Primary School, Upper Wortley

Brooklyn

B rilliant person
R eally good at drawing
O ranges are yucky
O vals are fun
K ai is the best
L ovely Mummy
Y ummy chocolate
N ice Daddy.

Brooklyn Lowther (6)
Five Lanes Primary School, Upper Wortley

Stanley

S o good at football
T igtastic!
A lways helps me
N ever shouts
L ikes pepperoni pizza
E ach day he works hard
Y our favourite colour is blue.

Leia Butler-Davis (6)
Five Lanes Primary School, Upper Wortley

Nurse

N urse a newborn baby
U se medical tools
R eady to work
S uper at taking care of patients
E nd of the day they will be tidy
S ort out, patients.

Ebony-Alice Tillett (7)

Five Lanes Primary School, Upper Wortley

Doctors

D octors are caring
O h, kind words
C aring hands
T he doctors are helpful
O n-time to the hospital
R eady for the day
S pecial.

Maria R (6)

Five Lanes Primary School, Upper Wortley

Harlow

H arlow is my sister
A mazing hugs
R emember she's only one
L ikes to play
O ver and over with her bear
W e play with the Barbie house!

Kassidy McGinlay (5)
Five Lanes Primary School, Upper Wortley

Callum

C allum gets up early
A nd he always watches YouTube
L oves me
L ets me play on the tablet
U sually, we get dressed up
M y brother Callum.

Jack Gregg (5)

Five Lanes Primary School, Upper Wortley

Doctors

D octors are good
O n calls
C aring for others
T hey're energetic
O h doctors are cool
R eady to help
S uperheroes.

Layton C (6)
Five Lanes Primary School, Upper Wortley

Super Doctor

D octors are caring
O ffer to help
C areful
T eaching
O ther doctors. Eat healthy
R eady for work
S tart to get tired.

Coral B (6)

Five Lanes Primary School, Upper Wortley

My Granny

G ives me sweets
R eads me books
A nd she gets me pizza
N ever stop being the best!
N ice dinner, Granny!
Y ou're great!

Sienna Hood (5)
Five Lanes Primary School, Upper Wortley

Domino

D reams of mice!
O nly eats cat food
M iaows quietly
I mportant part of my family
N ever goes camping!
O ften chases Dexter!

Theodore Gray (5)
Five Lanes Primary School, Upper Wortley

Doctors

D octors are helpful
O n the ball
C aring
T o help the amazing people
O pen
R eally kind
S uperhero.

Romahn Ali (6)
Five Lanes Primary School, Upper Wortley

Nurses

N urses are good
U nderstanding
R eally clever
S o they help sick people
E nsure people are good
S uperheroes.

Murray D (6)

Five Lanes Primary School, Upper Wortley

My Friend

L ikes to play tig
A lways kind to me
U sually very happy
R eally good friend
A nyway, you're a superstar!

Olivia Freeman (6)
Five Lanes Primary School, Upper Wortley

Doctors

D octors are caring
O n a train
C aring
T ake care
O utstanding
R eally kind
S pecial.

Rocco Whitaker (6)
Five Lanes Primary School, Upper Wortley

My Mummy

M y mummy is kind
U nderstands me and helps me
M ummy looks beautiful
M arvellous make-up
Y ou are the best!

Delilah Bailey (5)
Five Lanes Primary School, Upper Wortley

My Friend

A lways helps me
L oves to play with me at school
E veryone likes her
X tra nice
A sks me to be her friend.

Harriet Morley (5)

Five Lanes Primary School, Upper Wortley

Nurses

N urses are kind
U se tools to make people better
R espectful
S ensible
E xcellent
S ensitive.

Abigail Dickins (6)
Five Lanes Primary School, Upper Wortley

Doctors

D octors are good
O pen-minded
C aring
T rusting
O h, the best
R espectful
S afe.

Evelyn Nyachowe (6)
Five Lanes Primary School, Upper Wortley

Nurse

N ice and caring person
U nderstands his patients
R eally important
S aves lives
E very day he smiles.

Riley Austin Illingworth (6)
Five Lanes Primary School, Upper Wortley

Nurse

N ice and caring
U nderstanding people
R eally nice and smiley
S aving the world
E verything is sad.

Holly Trenholm (7)
Five Lanes Primary School, Upper Wortley

Mummy

M y mummy is amazing
U nique
M y mummy makes delicious food
M y mummy is amazing
Y oung and strong!

Lara Krakowska (6)
Five Lanes Primary School, Upper Wortley

Mummy

M y mummy makes me happy
U nique and strong
M y mummy is pretty
M any memories
Y oung and loves me!

Valentina Martins (6)

Five Lanes Primary School, Upper Wortley

Isaac

I saac plays with me
S illy Isaac language
A crazy little brother
A mazing running
C ute smile.

Isabella Raines (5)
Five Lanes Primary School, Upper Wortley

My Friend

M akes me happy
O ften plays with me
L oves her friends
L ikes cats
Y ou're very helpful.

Aaliyah Huffinley (5)

Five Lanes Primary School, Upper Wortley

Louie

L ittle brother
O ften plays darts
U nbelievably kind
I s good at Sonic Mania
E njoys books.

Liam Strutt (6)
Five Lanes Primary School, Upper Wortley

My Friend

C aring
A lways kind to me
S hows me how to play
E veryone likes him
Y ou're the best!

Edison Mitchell (5)
Five Lanes Primary School, Upper Wortley

Logan

L ogan is my brother
O reos are his favourite
G ood bike rider
A mazing writer
N ice.

Lexi Shaw (6)
Five Lanes Primary School, Upper Wortley

Tilly

T errific at maths
I mportant life
L oves people
L ovely
Y ellow flowers are amazing.

Tilly Wheelhouse (6)
Five Lanes Primary School, Upper Wortley

Daddy

D addy's hot chocolate
A good job
D ancing
D ark side watcher
Y ummy pancakes.

Leon Sharp (5)

Five Lanes Primary School, Upper Wortley

My Brother

T he youngest in my family
O ften giggles!
B lows bubbles a lot
Y esterday he made me laugh.

Theodore Mason (5)

Five Lanes Primary School, Upper Wortley

Nana

N ana is beautiful
A lways there for me
N ana watches films
A lways with treats!

Brogan Dargan (5)

Five Lanes Primary School, Upper Wortley

My Sister Lexi

L exi is my best friend
E veryone loves her
X tra special sister
I s amazing!

Logan Shaw (6)

Five Lanes Primary School, Upper Wortley

Casey

C hase me
A friend
S miles at me
E xtra nice
Y ou are kind.

Max Armitage (5)

Five Lanes Primary School, Upper Wortley

My Friend

E veryone loves you
S miley face
M akes me laugh
E xtra special friend.

Erynn Maloney (5)
Five Lanes Primary School, Upper Wortley

Mummy

M ummy is beautiful
U nique
M ummy is clever
M ummy
Y oung.

Willow Handley (5)
Five Lanes Primary School, Upper Wortley

Lily

L ily is my doll
I n my bedroom
L ittle and lovely
Y oung and sweet.

Isla Vause (5)

Five Lanes Primary School, Upper Wortley

Lexi

L exi is kind
E veryone plays with Lexi
X - pickles
I love her!

Ola Trebowicz (5)
Five Lanes Primary School, Upper Wortley

Lucas

L ucky kid
U nderstanding
C razy
A mazing
S pecial.

Lucas Garrett (7)

Five Lanes Primary School, Upper Wortley

Nyla

N ice
Y ou are nice
L ovely and helpful
A good person.

Layton Day (6)

Five Lanes Primary School, Upper Wortley

Sav

S he is smart and beautiful
A dorable and I love her
V ery funny!

Phoebe Wood (5)

Five Lanes Primary School, Upper Wortley

Mum

M y mum is beautiful
U nderstanding and nice
M y amazing mum.

Ellie Sykes (6)
Five Lanes Primary School, Upper Wortley

My Mum

M y mum is beautiful
U nbelievable cook!
M akes me happy.

Phoebe Seymour (5)
Five Lanes Primary School, Upper Wortley

Mum

M y mum loves me
U nderstanding
M y new cat is Pandora.

Dalton Monaghan-Fulthorpe (5)
Five Lanes Primary School, Upper Wortley

Mum

M akes me feel loved
U nique
M y mum is lovely.

Georgia Coneley (6)

Five Lanes Primary School, Upper Wortley

Max

M y friend
A kind boy
X - sprouts!

Bailey-James Butler (5)

Five Lanes Primary School, Upper Wortley

Winter

W hy is it cold?
I t's as cold as ice
N ow it is snowing
T he people are playing
E ach year it is getting colder
R ight, I'm going in now.

Scarlett Rose Artley (7)
Lily Park Primary Academy, Golcar

Snacks

S nacks are just the best
N ow I want to eat them
A lways yummy
C risps are crunchy
K eep them in a cupboard
S afe from my greedy brothers.

Ashlee Thomas (6)
Lily Park Primary Academy, Golcar

Hamster

H appy hamster
A soft, fluffy pet
M unching delicious food
S uch a nice pet
T iny paws
E njoys eating
R unning everywhere.

Lydia Shields (5)
Lily Park Primary Academy, Golcar

Mummy

M onday she brings me to super school
U nderstanding
M ummy gives cosy cuddles
M ummy gives caring kisses
Y ou are my pretty, helpful Mum.

Joshua Warner (6)
Lily Park Primary Academy, Golcar

Spiders

S piders are hairy
P laying outside
I n a web
D ark skin
E verywhere
R unning in a house
S neaking up behind you.

Aston Carr (7)

Lily Park Primary Academy, Golcar

Water

W ater is pouring out of the sink
A ll over the wet floor
T oday, water is everywhere
E veryone needs water
R ain gives us water.

Noah Bedford (6)
Lily Park Primary Academy, Golcar

Snakes

S lithering snakes
N ow up
A tree
K eeps on wriggling
E very day it's awake
S ometimes it sleeps at night.

Ben Dada (6)

Lily Park Primary Academy, Golcar

Pets

P ets are the best
E veryone must have one
T he hamster was so happy
S uch a cute, fluffy pet.

Mya Edwards (6)
Lily Park Primary Academy, Golcar

Dog

D elightful puppies
O pen mouth to bite a bone
G rowling at the terrified postman.

Ivy Woods (5)

Lily Park Primary Academy, Golcar

Dad

D ad drives a wagon
A lways plays with me
D oing Dad's stuff.

Jake Barber (6)

Lily Park Primary Academy, Golcar

Cat

C aring cat
A soft, fluffy kitten
T iny paws.

Scarlett-Rose Gray (5)

Lily Park Primary Academy, Golcar

Twinkerbell

T winkerbell is nice and kind
W illow loves Twinkerbell
I t's the best when she's at school
N ice is Twinkerbell's job
K ind all the time
E ggs are her favourite food
R eally kind when around
B eautiful
E veryone is kind to her
L itery looks like Twinkerbell
L ots of hugs from her.

Willow Searle (7)
Pen Mill Infant Academy, Yeovil

My Teacher

M iss Crawley is the best teacher
I like Miss Crawley
S he is the best
S uper smart

C rawley is her surname
R eally smiley teacher
A lways happy and well dressed
W e love you!
L oves to sing
E very day she dances
Y es, she is my favourite!

Daisy Shortland (6)
Pen Mill Infant Academy, Yeovil

Daddy

D addy likes to sleep a lot and he helps me
A ny day he likes to run outside with me
D ifferent days he likes to go to the shops
and get sweets
D uring the day we go to the hairdressers
Y uck my daddy gives me medicine.

Matei Nae (6)
Pen Mill Infant Academy, Yeovil

Brother

B rother is kind to me
R eally fun with me
O range is not his favourite fruit
T elevision is his favourite hobby
H appy all of the time
E very day we play
R eally love my brother.

Kuzey Ege Balci (7)
Pen Mill Infant Academy, Yeovil

My Mum's The Best

M ummy is the most kindest mum ever
U pstairs she makes surprises for me
M ummy helps me get stuff from the cupboards
M y mum is very important to me
Y esterday for dinner we had pizza.

Sienna Johnstone (6)
Pen Mill Infant Academy, Yeovil

My Parrot

A rchie is the best
R ats go in his cage!
C ows follow Archie when he goes out
H e sleeps on a cage bar
I love Archie because he is the best!
E ven Archie swears!

Ceejay Ball (7)
Pen Mill Infant Academy, Yeovil

Hollymay

H ollymay is kind to me
O n the playground
L ovely girl
L ike me
Y ou are the funniest
M y friend
A mazing at maths
Y ou are my best buddy.

Eli Martin (6)
Pen Mill Infant Academy, Yeovil

Harry

H arry is my best friend
A lways kind
R unning is healthy so me and Harry
R un, "It is pouring down," I said to Harry
Y ummy ice cream I feed to Harry.

Hanna Bialek (6)
Pen Mill Infant Academy, Yeovil

Kacper

K acper plays with me at playtime
A mazing Kacper
C aring Kacper
P eople think Kacper is funny
E veryone thinks Kacper is the best
R unning Kacper.

Dawid Piekaz (6)
Pen Mill Infant Academy, Yeovil

Fluffy

F luffy is small
L ike to play with Fluffy
U pstairs is out of bounds
F luffy is cute
F luffy is fun
Y es, Fluffy is my favourite!

Maisy Ellis (6)
Pen Mill Infant Academy, Yeovil

My Fox

M y fox is my best friend
Y ellow eyes, little bit of black

F luffy and furry
O range fur
X ylophone is her favourite instrument.

Charlotte Wright (6)
Pen Mill Infant Academy, Yeovil

Mummy

M ummy always gives me the best
U nicorns are my mum's favourite
M ummy loves me
M ummy plays Minecraft with me
Y ummy dinners.

Maddison Speechley (6)
Pen Mill Infant Academy, Yeovil

My Mummy

M y mummy is the best
U mmm, Mummy wakes me up
M y mummy works at Art Space
M y mummy has brown hair
Y ay, my mummy plays with me!

Salome Dubos (6)
Pen Mill Infant Academy, Yeovil

Matei

M y friend is a wellbeing
A mbassador in Owl class
T akes turns in Duck, Duck, Goose
E ats school lunch
I s a good friend.

Melodie McCarthy (6)

Pen Mill Infant Academy, Yeovil

Ky-Mani

K y-Mani you are good
Y ou are good at games

M y friend
A lovely time
N ice boy he is
I like you.

Alfie Foster (6)
Pen Mill Infant Academy, Yeovil

Daddy

D addy cuddles me
A mazing Daddy
D addy cooks me pie and chips
D addy has a cup of tea
Y ou are the best!

Mia-May Evans (6)
Pen Mill Infant Academy, Yeovil

Mummy

M ummy is nice
U ndeniably beautiful
M ummy gives me cuddles
M ummy loves me
Y ou are the best!

Aviela Bearneza (6)
Pen Mill Infant Academy, Yeovil

Holly

H olly is kind
O h you are a star
L ikes to play with me
L oves me
Y ou are the best!

Lexi Warren (6)
Pen Mill Infant Academy, Yeovil

Theeo

T heeo is kind
H e is clever
E xciting games
E xcellent rating
O h, you are great!

Arya Amber (6)
Pen Mill Infant Academy, Yeovil

Beth

B eth is amazing
E specially at games
T he best sister today
H er hair is pretty.

Reuben Smith (6)
Pen Mill Infant Academy, Yeovil

Mammy

M ammy is kind
A lways plays with
M e with cars
M akes it fun
Y es!

Daniel Whitt (6)
Pen Mill Infant Academy, Yeovil

Arya

A rya plays games with me
R eally fun
Y ou are lovely
A rya is my friend.

Theeo Woolley (7)
Pen Mill Infant Academy, Yeovil

Harvest

H appy festival everybody!
A lovely day for a pick
R ed, juicy strawberries are ready to be picked!
V egetables are the best you can ever eat
E verybody loves delicious fruit and vegetables
S end fruit to everybody!
T hen everybody is going to be happy again!

Aayat-Noor Khan (6)
Riverside Primary School, Barking

Harvest

H appy harvest is here!
A scrumptious apple is here for everybody
R ed, lovely strawberries are finally ready
V eggies are the best food ever!
E verybody loves eating healthy fruit
S trawberries are the juiciest fruit ever
T asty fruits are finally here.

Zara Asad (6)
Riverside Primary School, Barking

Harvest

H arvest time everybody!
A pples and sweet strawberries for
everyone!
R ace to harvest again!
V eggies for everyone
E very poor child, we're here
S tay, we need you for harvest
T ell the poor we have apples.

King II Chukwuedo (7)
Riverside Primary School, Barking

Harvest

H appy harvest once again!
A pples are scrumptious and red
R ipe crops being picked by farmers
V ery poor people need food too
E verybody loves vegetables
S ending baskets of food
T oday is a special day.

Amelia-Mae Moyosore Akindele (7)
Riverside Primary School, Barking

Harvest

H appy harvest day to all
A pples are delicious and fruity
R ipe crops ready to be picked
V ery poor people need food too
E veryone likes fruit and veggies
S preading love to the world
T ime to celebrate!

Alessia Simoes Ohaekebosi (7)
Riverside Primary School, Barking

Harvest

H ealthy harvest is here!
A pple harvest is here
R ipe crops are ready to be picked
V egetables are delicious
E verybody loves eating vegetables
S ending fruit to poor people
T he people are happy.

Isabel Peprah (7)
Riverside Primary School, Barking

Harvest

H appy people love fruit!
A pples are delicious
R ed, lovely radishes
V egetables are scrumptious
E verything is amazing
S trawberries are a little bit sour
T he yummy vegetables.

Zoe Pui Yi Lee (6)
Riverside Primary School, Barking

Leaf

L eaves fall down
E verywhere is beautiful
A utumn leaves change colour
F alling leaves blow in the wind.

Mckinley-Rose Asak (5)
Riverside Primary School, Barking

Leaf

L eaves are falling from trees
E verything is colourful
A ll the leaves are crunchy
F alling all around.

Ivy Neriya (6)
Riverside Primary School, Barking

Amazing Jason

A mazing, smart, my cousin is brave
M akes me happy and sometimes we play football
A kind person, his age is 16
Z ebras are his favourite thing to talk about
I like him, he is also handsome
N ewspapers were his favourite thing when he was a child
G ood and sometimes he is so lazy

J uice, he does not like juice
A cting, when he started school he was acting
S o much he wants to go around the world
O ur show and tell was awesome, he brought some cakes
N on-fiction, he loves it, he reads it to me.

Kevin Wireko (6)
St Joseph's Catholic Infant School, Leyton

Cutest Sasha

C ute, furry and cuddly
U s, we think she is sometimes naughty
T he kittens of Sasha have been taken away
E very day we feed her
S asha is so cute!
T he food that she likes most is dry!

S asha is great at cuddling up!
A lazy cat sometimes!
S he is a very active cat!
H er toy mouse is blue!
A n adventurous cat, of course!

Gioia Piras (6)
St Joseph's Catholic Infant School, Leyton

Lovely Sister

L ove you sister! You are the cutest to me
O f course, you are lovely Cian
V ery good at eating vegetables
E xciting picture, I love it so much
L earning hard
Y ou wear beautiful dresses

S o you look beautiful
I t is lovely
S ister, you are a pretty sister
T his is so nice
E very day happy
R eally caring.

Nyah Robinson (6)
St Joseph's Catholic Infant School, Leyton

Amazing Mum

A lways kind to me
M y mummy gives me healthy food
A lways loves me
Z oo is her favourite place
I like when she takes me to parks
N ever breaks the law
G ood every day

M ummy is the best
U nkind people don't like her
M ummy doesn't like when they don't like her.

Oscar Vazquez Danielewicz (6)
St Joseph's Catholic Infant School, Leyton

My Best Daddy

M akes me joyful
Y ummy food he makes

B rave dad
E xhausted after work
S ing very funny
T eaches me new things sometimes

D ad makes jokes and he has books
A wonderful man he is
D ances and he makes me laugh
D ad plays a lot with me
Y awns when he sleeps.

Denis Patras (6)
St Joseph's Catholic Infant School, Leyton

Best Cousin

B est cousin
E xcellent, she makes me laugh
S ings me songs
T alent

C ute and careful
O ctober, on Halloween she dressed like a witch
U p she climbed on a slide
S he dances with me
I n her home, she has a trampoline
N ear her friend's home, there was a baby, so cute.

Khanishna Moorghen (6)
St Joseph's Catholic Infant School, Leyton

Best Cousin

B eautiful, smart, kind and amazing
E ffort they make and they cheer me up
S pecial, creative
T eaches me

C alls me when I am lonely
O n reading her book
U sually always happy
S miling every day
I nspirational
N othing can separate us.

Christine Duarte Joseph (6)
St Joseph's Catholic Infant School, Leyton

My Poem About Mummy

M y mum cares for me very much, she is loving and kind
U nderstands me when I speak Polish and French
M y mum plays games with me like a pro gamer and a pixel gamer
M y mum loves me very much and she is very funny
Y ummy food my mum cooks for me every time to stay healthy and fit.

Klaudia Pacyna (6)

St Joseph's Catholic Infant School, Leyton

Grandma

G reat at baking cookies
R eading clearly at bedtime
A mazing at doing puppets
N ever gives up on her hard work
D reaming and hugging me to keep me
warm
M arvellous at making jokes up!
A nd helps sick and ill people that are old!

Ava Lewis (6)
St Joseph's Catholic Infant School, Leyton

Jack Robisan

J olly good
A mazing
C aring for me
K ind to everyone

R eally good
O ne condition - he is the best!
B est at biting
I t's genius
S o good
A superstar
N ever stops biting.

Jack Breeden (6)
St Joseph's Catholic Infant School, Leyton

Mummy

M y mum is so nice and kind
Y ummy food that she makes and is mine

M y mummy is so beautiful
U nderstanding how to learn
M y mummy is so happy, nice and lovely
M y mummy is so amazing
Y ummy, yummy food my mum makes.

Azarni Williams-Cox (6)
St Joseph's Catholic Infant School, Leyton

Teacher

T eachers are kind
E xcellent learning in the school
A mazing teaching in the school
C aring, wonderful and really cool
H appy and helpful to everyone
E veryone is enthusiastic when they teach
R esilient, talented teachers!

Matteo Sarcone (7)
St Joseph's Catholic Infant School, Leyton

My Brother

M y brave brother
Y ou are the best

B eing helpful to me
R unning with me
O h, he is the best brother
T eaching me to ride a bike
H elping me
E ating my best food
R acing with me today.

Malachi Sserwadda (7)

St Joseph's Catholic Infant School, Leyton

My Poem About My Dad

D ads are kind and use their minds
A dad is clever and is always better
D ads are fast and always a blast
D addy helps me when I am stuck
Y ummy food my daddy makes and he
makes me want to bake a cake.

Anastasios Goodchild (6)
St Joseph's Catholic Infant School, Leyton

Best Dad

B est dad
E ats vegetables
S tays at home
T eaches me to be a good grown-up

D ad doesn't get angry at me
A mazing dad
D ad is a good person.

Prince Donkor (6)
St Joseph's Catholic Infant School, Leyton

Mummy

M ummy is the best
U nderstanding how to be a teacher
M ummy is the best because I love her
M ummy is the best because I love her
Y ummy food that my mummy makes.

Martyn Molina Santos (6)
St Joseph's Catholic Infant School, Leyton

My Mummy

M y mummy is amazing at maths
U nderstands and listens to me
M y mummy is beautiful and kind
M y mummy helps me with maths
Y ummy dinners my mummy makes!

Annabel Nogalers (6)
St Joseph's Catholic Infant School, Leyton

My Poem About A Nurse

N ice and kind nurse
U nderstands what people say
R ushing on their work and things they do
S aying polite things
E xcellent things she does!

Marivic Siscar (6)
St Joseph's Catholic Infant School, Leyton

My Dog Angel

A dorable face
N eeding food all the time
G olden hair
E asily excited
L ovely and loving.

David Richards (7)
The King's House School, Windsor

My Saella

S weet
A mazing
E xcellent
L oyal
L ikeable
A dmirable.

Garrett Lamos (6)
The King's House School, Windsor

David's Achievement

D etermined
A mazing
V irtuous
I ntelligent
D edicated.

Johan Gonowathrer (6)

The King's House School, Windsor

My Amazing Nannie

A mazing Nannie
M y nan is really kind
A lso, she is extremely beautiful
Z ooming around the kitchen
I n her little red apron
N annie loves to cook
G lowing skin, you would never guess her age

N annie is spectacular
A theltic she is not but...
N annie is amazing.

Elise Chalmers (6)
Whittle Academy, Walsgrave

Forest

F oggy morning
O wls sleeping
R unning deer playing
E agles eating worms
S nakes slithering
T rees blocking our way.

Pranesh Dineshkumar (7)
Whittle Academy, Walsgrave

Lakshana

L akshana
A ngel
K ind
S hasha
H airdresser
A ntarctica
N ight
A thletics.

Shasha Sakthivel (6)
Whittle Academy, Walsgrave

The Dog

D og is digging mud
O range ball is her favourite toy
G orgeous dog is kind.

Timur Kiselovs (6)
Whittle Academy, Walsgrave

The Giraffes

G inormous giraffe stands tall
I n the savannah looking cool
R ubbing its bum against the trees
A ngrily getting rid of its fleas
F leas jump off in a hurry
F alling to the ground and off they scurry
E lephant stamps with every tread
S quashing the fleas and turning them red.

Rupert Boxall (6)
Wigmore Primary School, Wigmore

Christian

C hristian is funny
H e's a boy
R ock, rock strong
I am his brother
S it on the chair
T alks with me
I like him
A cting in a film
N ice to everyone.

Victor Vatahov (5)
Wigmore Primary School, Wigmore

My Best Friend

W oody is my best friend
O ne day we went for a walk
O h look a snail
D on't eat the snail Woody
Y ou're a good boy.

Nellie Powell (5)

Wigmore Primary School, Wigmore

My Mummy

M agnificent
Y appy

M ad
U nderstanding
M arvellous
M odest
Y oung at heart.

Eira Wyn Gibson (5)
Wigmore Primary School, Wigmore

Mossy Dog

M y dog
O bedient
S haggy
S oft
Y aps

D ear
O ld
G rey

Isobel Salmon (5)
Wigmore Primary School, Wigmore

Meerkat

M onkeying around
E ars
E at
R un
K icking
A ttention
T unnel.

Ted Tomlinson (5)
Wigmore Primary School, Wigmore

My Kind, Helpful Teachers

T oday we love our teachers
E very day we will give you a flower
A t school, our teachers care for us
C aring for us, we care for you
H appy to learn and good handwriting
E nglish, maths, science and others
R ewards for getting high scores
S chool is the best.

Xzavier Smith (6)
Windmill Hill Primary School, Windmill Hill

My Kind, Noisy Brothers

B rothers are so nice
R eally funny and happy
O reos are Dylan's favourite snack
T hey're very nice
H ear my baby brother cry
E veryone loves my baby brother
R esting eyes and rosy cheeks
S weet and cute.

Oliver Jenkins (7)

Windmill Hill Primary School, Windmill Hill

My Kind, Helpful Teachers

T he day starts with a big smile
E ach day everybody learns
A lways be kind
C lever teachers
H elpful teachers
E ach teacher is the best
R eally kind teachers
S aturday and Sunday are our days to rest.

Marley Pickup (6)
Windmill Hill Primary School, Windmill Hill

Friends

F unny and thoughtful
R eally helpful
I nteresting friend
E very day we play together
N ever usually argue
D oughnuts we love to eat
S o much fun with my friend.

Esmae Sheldon (7)
Windmill Hill Primary School, Windmill Hill

Tilly, My Lovely, Beautiful Friend

F riendly and she has pink hair
R eally good at knitting
I love her, she is beautiful
E veryone thinks she is funny
N ice and helpful
D ogs are her favourite animal.

Tilly Heatley (7)
Windmill Hill Primary School, Windmill Hill

A Helpful, Kind Grandad

G randad is the best
R eally kind
A good person
N ice and happy
D ogs are his favourite animal
A lways helpful
D oes lots of things with me.

Olly Poole (7)

Windmill Hill Primary School, Windmill Hill

My Helpful, Beautiful Sister

S o my sister is the best
I love my sister
S illy and funny
T ake your time with your homework
E very day my sister is nice to me
R eally kind.

Natalia Dowolska (6)
Windmill Hill Primary School, Windmill Hill

My Sister Is Kind And Helpful

S he loves me so much
I love her back so much
S he laughs so much
T ogether we play
E veryone loves her
R eally kind and cuddly.

Hannah Holliday (7)
Windmill Hill Primary School, Windmill Hill

My Pretty Mum

M y mum makes me happy
Y ou cook me vegetables

M akes me pasta
U nderstands me
M y mum is the best.

Cheyenne Jones (6)
Windmill Hill Primary School, Windmill Hill

My Kind, Nice Daddy

D addy, I love you
A lways cool
D oughnuts he loves
D addy makes me smile
Y ou are nice to me.

Cecelia Fenwick (7)
Windmill Hill Primary School, Windmill Hill

My Kind Nicky

N icky is friendly
I love Nicky so much
C uddles are the best
K ind and happy
Y ou love me.

Anton Rooney (6)

Windmill Hill Primary School, Windmill Hill

Mum

M akes me smile
U nderstands me
M ummy loves me and I love her.

Deacon Seston (6)

Windmill Hill Primary School, Windmill Hill

Young Writers Information

We hope you have enjoyed reading this book – and that you will continue to in the coming years.

If you're a young writer who enjoys reading and creative writing, or the parent of an enthusiastic poet or story writer, do visit our website **www.youngwriters.co.uk**. Here you will find free competitions, workshops and games, as well as recommended reads, a poetry glossary and our blog. There's lots to keep budding writers motivated to write!

If you would like to order further copies of this book, or any of our other titles, then please give us a call or order via your online account.

Young Writers
Remus House
Coltsfoot Drive
Peterborough
PE2 9BF
(01733) 890066
info@youngwriters.co.uk

Join in the conversation!
Tips, news, giveaways and much more!

YoungWritersUK **@YoungWritersCW**